Paw Prints
in the
Somme

By Dan Metcalf

To Sheba, Chunky & Posy.
Thanks for the purrs.

Author's Note

During the First World War, it is estimated that 500,000 cats were sent to the trenches of France and Belgium.

This is the story of just one.

Dan Metcalf

Chapter One

Lock Eyes, Sink Low

The screech of the cat's call echoed off the wall of the barn. Tom bounced out of his hiding place and leapt at the ball of grey fur on the ground. He was six months old now; small and lean but his kittenish movements made him look ungainly, clumsy even. His limbs flailed as he leapt through the air, a blur of orange fur.

The mouse looked up, seemingly unconcerned. It took a moment to look at Tom, as if to say 'not *you* again,' before it trotted away under a hay bale.

Tom landed at the spot where the mouse had been with a thump, hitting his pointy ginger chin on the ground. His paws clattered down on the cold floor and failed to stop the rest of his body as he fell in a heap. He shook his head to clear the stars surrounding him.

"Ha-ha!" came a laugh from above. The crows in the rafters were in stitches. "Keep tryin' young'un!" called one of the birds. "Practice makes perfect!"

"In his case, it'll make a broken leg," said another crow. The flock collapsed into hysterics again.

"Shut up, you lot!" called Tom. His voice was thin, his kitten's mew not yet developed into a cat's growl. "Or you'll be next!"

"Oooooooohh! Big words, little cat!" called the leader. "You'll hafta catch us first!"

Tom sat up straight, licked his paw and wet the fur on his head before walking out into the sunshine.

The courtyard of the farm was bathed in light and Tom emerged from the barn, blinking. He could hear the lowing of the cows in the nearby fields that told him it was nearly milking time. He might have time to wander by the sheds to see if Old Jack had any cream to spare…

"How did it go, darling?"

The voice made Tom jump. He looked up to see his mother, Jezebel, lying in a sunbeam on top of a water butt.

"Um...nearly got him this time," said Tom. He didn't even convince himself. "But he kind of...got away."

Jezebel rose and stretched, arching her back and making the fur on her tail stand up straight. She leapt down to the ground with grace and poise.

"Then we'll go through it again, my dear."

"But Mum, I-" Tom's protests were stopped by a look which told him that Jezebel would take no arguments.

She glanced at a dandelion that had risen up through the cracks in the courtyard. This was the target. She walked away and turned.

"Remember, stealth is silence," she whispered. "Turn and see your target. Lock eyes on it and do not look away even for a moment. Crouch down low."

Jezebel lowered her body to the ground and kept her gaze on the yellow flower. She began to crawl forward.

"Approach your target. Once you are within a few paces, take aim. Wiggle your bottom-" Tom let out a snort. That part always made him laugh.

"Focus, young Tom!" A voice chided him from across the courtyard. Stanley, a black and white brute of a cat, approached. He was old and his spine was visible through his black coat, but his size still made him a force to be reckoned with on the farm. "If you don't concentrate, you'll never learn."

Jezebel raised her bottom once more and moved it from side to side. She then used her powerful hind legs to spring herself forward and grab the head of the dandelion between her two front paws.

"Stretch your claws. That should stop them writhing," said Jezebel. A few stray petals fell to the ground as she demonstrated. "Or sink your teeth in."

"Is that how you did it, Tom? In the barn?" asked Stanley, his deep voice cracking with age.

"Yes. Almost," said Tom. "Everything apart from the eye contact. And the silence." The withering looks from his mother and Stanley made him feel ashamed. Stanley had been like a father to him, taught him everything a mouser needed to know. The only trouble was that Tom had rarely paid attention. "I'll keep trying. I'll get it right."

Old Jack rounded the corner with a milk pail, on his way to the milking shed. He looked tired. The farm was a lot to manage at his age. He had the eggs to collect, cows to milk, animals to feed and a trip to market each week. He still took time to stop and stroke each cat on his way.

"What are you three planning? World domination, no doubt!" he joked. He put his large, rough finger under Tom's chin and stroked. Tom purred as if he were going to explode with delight. "And what of young Tom? Is he a great mouser yet?" he said. "Listen to these two and you'll go far, my lad."

He trudged off in muddy boots towards the sheds.

"See?" said Jezebel. "Old Jack has faith in you."

"And you owe him your life, remember," said Stanley. "Jack kept you alive when most of your litter had perished. He fed you and gave you shelter."

"I know, I know," said Tom. "I'll get the hang of it."

Stanley was right. He felt an enormous sense of gratitude towards Old Jack and wanted to do him proud. Looking at his size, Tom was obviously the runt of the litter but against all odds had survived when his siblings had not. He walked out into the meadow with purpose, into the long grass.

"Lock eyes. Sink low. Wiggle bum – pounce!" he recited. "Lock eyes. Sink low. Wiggle bum – pounce!"

The meadow became his practice area, his hunting ground. He played until sunset and beyond everyday, hunting flowers, butterflies, shadows and moths.

Until one day, when a harvest mouse appeared. It hung delicately from a tall blade of grass, its tail curled around the stem. *It's so small,* thought Tom. Smaller than the mice in the barn and even those had evaded him so far. He wasn't afraid of hunting it. If anything, he was eager. He wasn't precious about killing it either. He knew that any mouse had to be dealt with immediately, or they would breed and destroy the crops altogether. If he hesitated then it was for one reason only; fear of failure.

If he could not pounce a tiny harvest mouse then what good was he to Old Jack? What would Jezebel and Stanley say? Would the ever-watching crows laugh again?

He had frozen for just a moment but he made himself snap out of it. He ran himself through the list he knew by heart.

Lock eyes.

He set his sights on the mouse, maintaining his silence.

Sink low.

Tom lowered his body to the ground, his chin resting on his paws.

Wiggle bum.

His behind rose in the air and shifted from side to side.

Pounce!

He leapt! He kept his eyes on the mouse, which did not even turn to see him. Tom sandwiched it between his paws and landed with a splat on the ground. Tom felt a brief wriggle under his paws which ended as soon as he flexed his claws.

Just like Mum said it would, he thought.

He raised his paw to look at the dead mouse. It was a small rodent, but a huge victory. He ran back to the farmyard as quickly as his paws could carry him, the mouse between his teeth.

When he arrived there, Jezebel was nowhere to be seen. Nor Stanley. They were probably shading themselves in the barn from the unreasonably hot Devon sun. He started to walk towards the barn but heard footsteps around the corner. Old Jack came into the yard, his pitchfork in hand.

"Good afternoon, Master Thomas," he said, mock-formal. He stopped and looked closer at the kitten's mouth. "What you got there then my lover?" The old man smiled as Tom dropped his prize at his feet. "Well I'll be! He's a mouser after all!"

Chapter Two

Instinct

Tom soon became a master mouser. He threw himself into his role, patrolling the yard everyday, peering into nooks and crannies to find the rodents' hiding places.

"There he goes! King of Hill Farm!" yelled Stanley from his comfortable position in the sun. He was old and welcomed the chance to retire. While other cats may have been threatened by a kitten taking over their job, Stanley stood back gratefully and let Tom get on with it. Tom smiled at the old man as he trotted by, head held high.

It was just past midday, the sun high in the sky. Tom ran up to Jezebel who was dozing in the shade. The hay under her body was flat from lying on it and it looked like a small nest for a cat.

"What should I do now, Mum?" Tom said eagerly. Jezebel looked up dozily.

"Hmm? Have you done the courtyard?"

"Yes! Tom announced proudly.

"And the milking sheds?"

"Yes! And I didn't even drink the cream!"

"Good boy. What about the hay store?"

"Not yet! I'll do it now," he said before bounding away. He ran through the farm in a blur of orange fur, sending the hens into a flurry of feathers.

"Slow down, young Tom!" they clucked disapprovingly.

"Sorry ladies!" Tom called back. "Work to do!" He dashed into the hay store, a stone building with a slate roof and no door. It was dark and cool inside. The sun was high, so the only light peeked in through small holes in the roof, dust floating through the sunbeams. Tom stopped a few yards away and tried to look inside. He had not patrolled the hay store before and was wary of places he did not know. He knew all the mouse holes in the yard and main barn, all the hiding places a rodent might lurk. When faced with an unknown area, he liked to take his time. "No hurry," he said to himself. "Stealth is silence..."

Tom crept gingerly up to the doorway and peeked inside. It was midsummer and Old Jack had yet to harvest more hay. The store was down to its last few bales. They were stacked up against the back wall, with hay strewn around the floor.

Tom felt his heart beat faster. He did not like the dark. He did not know why; maybe it was primal, but part of him was screaming at him to run.

But he had a job to do and could not let Jezebel down. He had to look, wait and pounce on any rodents in there. He wanted Old Jack to be proud of him. He approached the bales.

From the corner of his eye he saw a flick of a pink tale disappear behind the hay. He stopped mid-prowl and turned his head.

That looked big, thought Tom. *Really big. Jack'll be proud for sure if I bring him a mouse like that!*

Slowly he prowled towards it, staying silent. He needed the element of surprise.

A nest of sparrows in the rafters suddenly took flight, whizzing low past Tom and startling him. He let out a small mew in shock.

Drat! he thought. *So much for a surprise attack.*

He heard a rustle in the bales. His prey had definitely heard him. Whereas the mice he had encountered before would normally squeak and scuttle away, this one stayed. It moved slightly, until Tom could see the slightest hint of a pink nose peeking out around the corner.

Get ready, he thought. *Lock eyes. Sink low. Wiggle bum...*

The nose peeked out further to reveal long whiskers each side. It sniffed and was followed around the corner by a large black head. Two red eyes stared back at Tom and he froze.

A rat.

A huge, black rat.

It was almost as big as Tom. It sniffed again and bared its razor sharp white teeth.

Tom ran.

He darted back through the yard, sending the hens flapping once more and coming to an abrupt stop outside the stables, where Stanley was cleaning himself.

"RAT! RAT!" shouted Tom.

"Where?" said Stanley, suddenly rising, preparing to pounce.

"In the hay store!"

"Did you get it? It's never enough to just claw them, Tom. You've got to bite the blighters as well or they'll come back fighting."

"I...I..." stammered Tom. He looked down, ashamed. "I ran."

Stanley was quiet for a moment. Tom hated the silence. He just wanted Stanley to tell him off and be done with it.

"I'll deal with it," he said. He stretched his legs and his old bones creaked. He set off towards the hay store at little more than a strolling pace. He turned back to Tom before he left the courtyard. "Rats are formidable foes, young Tom. Nothing like mice. But if you are to prove yourself of use on this farm you'd better toughen up and learn to kill 'em. Or Old Jack will have no choice but to give you away."

Later, Stanley limped back into the yard, covered in scratches and blood.

"Stanley!" screamed Jezebel. "What are you playing at, going after a rat at your age?"

"Piff!" Stanley said. "My age, indeed! I've still got a bit of fight left in me." He began to laugh.

"So...this blood," said Tom. "It's not yours?" Stanley looked down at himself.

"Some of it, maybe," he said. He smiled, his eyes twinkling with mischief. "But you should see the other fella..."

Tom sighed as Stanley lay down to rest. He was a coward. If he hadn't run, Stanley wouldn't have been hurt.

Later that night as dusk pulled in, he curled up with Jezebel. She sniffed him and gently closed her eyes, purring; a cat's kiss.

"Mum, why did I run?"

"Run, dear?" she said. She purred and licked his head. "I expect it was instinct."

"What's that?" Tom said.

"Instinct? It's the most important thing in a cat's life. It's the feeling you get when you know you *have* to do something. You don't know *why*, you just know that you *have* to."

Tom thought.

"Is it always right?" he asked. Jezebel laughed.

"Yes, most of the time. It's only when you stop to question it that things can go wrong. Take the rat," she said. Tom shuddered at the memory of its oily-looking black fur and its red eyes. "Your instinct told you to run. You knew, deep down, that you were too small to fight it. If you had not trusted your instinct and stayed put, maybe you would have lost the fight. Because you *did* trust it, you escaped unharmed."

The barn was fully dark now, with just the buzzing sound of crickets in the field to keep Jezebel and Tom company.

"So I should always trust my instincts?" asked Tom.

"Sometimes it's all you have," said Jezebel sleepily. "Now go to sleep. It's late."

"Yes, Mum," said Tom. "G'night."

"Sweet dreams, angel kitten."

Chapter Three

Stranger at Hill Farm

Old Jack was pulling a cart of manure through the farmyard when the soldier arrived. It was an officer on horseback. Jack had heard him coming up the lane but assumed it was his neighbour riding down to market in Crediton.

The officer, a captain by the look of the three pips on his shoulder, brought his grand black stallion to a halt in the yard. He stayed in the saddle, looking down from his unfair vantage point at Jack from below his peaked green cap. Jack stopped dead.

"Good day, Sir!" the captain said, nodding to Old Jack. He had a city accent; short and clipped.

"If you say so," said Jack brusquely. He stood dead still, staring at the captain with a look of hatred. Unperturbed by his silence, the captain continued.

"I am Captain Andrews of the Devonshire Regiment," he said. "I've been in the village talking to the locals. We are recruiting more men for our battalions fighting in Northern France. You know of our efforts in the war?"

Jack stayed put. His look of contempt was unwavering.

"I'm very aware," he said quietly.

"Then I wondered if I could speak to the young men on your farm. Farmhands, or your son perhaps?"

Old Jack slowly shook his head.

This wrong-footed Andrews slightly. He was not used to being told 'no' in his position. He adjusted his cap, cleared his throat and reigned in his horse, who had got bored and begun to wander towards a tasty looking bale of straw.

"I'll, um, remind you that it is your civic duty to help the war effort any way you can."

Old Jack curled his hand into a fist.

"You want young men? They're gone. All of 'em," said Old Jack. His voice was shaking. "My boy signed up as soon as the fighting began. Promised he'd be home by Christmas, he did. Then we gets a telegram."

Captain Andrews looked down.

"I'm sorry for your loss. I-"

"It destroyed us," Jack continued. "His Ma took to her bed. She was gone within a month n'all. Doctor said it was a broken heart."

Tom had been lazing in the sunshine for a while but Jack's voice had grown too loud to ignore. He lifted his head and went to see what all the fuss was about.

"Then you introduced the draft. One by one you called up my farmhands. They were good men. Then it were just me left. This place all to myself."

Tom walked up and mewed, rubbing his body against Old Jack's legs, though Jack was too angry to notice or return the affection.

"They even took my horse."

"And His Majesty is very grateful. The fact remains that the war is still in progress. Our men are risking their lives on the front line in France and Belgium. Your country needs help old man. You should give all you can."

Old Jack threw down his shovel and briskly walked up to the soldier. The horse immediately tried to back away, sensing danger, but Andrews reigned him in. Jack was red-faced, his eyes wide with anger.

"Haven't I given enough?" he spat. The two men stared at each other for a time. Jack eventually backed away. He turned to leave.

"They're bringing in mousers to the trenches," said Captain Andrews. He nodded to Tom who was sat in the middle of the courtyard, washing his hind leg. His paw was stretched to the sky like a ballerina. He looked up as if curious as to why they were both looking at him.

Jack looked at the officer, agog.

"You'd take my cat as well?" he said.

"My orders are to collect personnel for the front line. That now includes cats," Captain Andrews said matter-of-factly. His expression was blank, unapologetic.

Old Jack looked from the soldier to Tom and then back again.

"He...he's just a kitten," he said under his breath.

"Can it hunt?" asked Andrews. Jack hesitated.

"Yes, but..."

"Then hand it over," Andrews snapped. "It'll
be an asset to the regiment. Mice are taking the
trenches over and spreading disease. Your cat can
be of service."

Jack's blood boiled. He held his fist by his
side. He longed to throw a punch at the rude, un-
caring soldier but he saw the service revolver on
his side, the holster unclipped. If he attacked a soldier in the British Army, Andrews would be well
within his rights to fire in self defense. Instead, Jack
marched to the house and brought out an old,
small crate.

He walked back to the yard and picked up
Tom, who gave an involuntary mew. In the barn,
Jezebel's ears pricked up.

"Something's happening," she whispered.
"Tom!"

She darted out into the courtyard, followed
by a sleepy Stanley.

"Mum!" cried Tom as Old Jack tried to put him in the crate. "Mum! What's happening?" Tom put his paws on the edges to stop himself being pushed in, but Old Jack was used to handling horses and cows and was much stronger.

Tom landed in the crate and looked up at Old Jack, whose eyes were red with regret. He reached down and touched Tom's collar.

"You come back to me this time, Tom." He reached into his pocket and pulled out something he hadn't parted with in two years. A metal disc with words stamped on it. He attached it to Tom's collar and gave his head one last stroke. Jack closed the lid. The crate was small but had holes in it which Tom peeked through. He let out the loudest mew he could manage and Jezebel came bounding across the yard. Old Jack placed the crate down on the ground so his mother could give him one last sniff.

"Where am I going, Mum?" said Tom, on the verge of panicking. "What did I do wrong?"

"Nothing my darling boy!" said Jezebel. "It's just your new life beginning. Just be good, serve your master and remember everything we taught you."

Stanley did not come near, but instead nodded curtly to Tom.

"Head up, young Tom. You're a fine mouser. Be proud."

Tom poked a paw through the thin slats of the crate and Jezebel gave it a single lick before Old Jack lifted him again and gave him to Captain Andrews.

"You never come back here again, y'hear? Ever."

Tom was strapped onto the saddle and pushed his nose through the small air hole. He peered out as the horse trotted away. He watched as his home, his family and his master disappeared from view. Soon all he could hear was his mother yelling one final piece of advice.

"Remember Tom! Trust your instinct!"

Chapter Four

Tom's War

Lost, frightened and alone, Tom's war had begun. He didn't know where he was, where he was going or whether he would return to Hill Farm. All he knew now was the dark and cold as he was transported to what everyone seemed to call 'The Front'.

Tom had been transferred into a cage in the town near his farm and then loaded onto the back of a cart. The ride was less bumpy from that point, but only slightly.

"Hello?" Tom mewed. "Does anyone know where we're going?"

He could see other figures in cages in the half-dark but each was sleeping or curled up into a ball and steadfastly ignoring him. "Someone must know!" Tom shrieked.

"No one knows," said a gruff voice in the dark below him. "If we did, what good would it do? We'll know where we're going when we get there."

"B-but," stammered Tom.

"But nuffin," said the voice. "Go to sleep."

Tom was not exactly comforted by this but it was better than shouting at the darkness and hearing nothing back. He was at least comforted by the thought that the darkness *could* answer, if it wanted to. He slept.

*

The bumps of the cart gave way to the fluid up and down motion of a boat. Locked in a dark hold, many of the cats in the cages were ill. Tom could hear them retching and coughing but could do nothing to save himself. He could hear it and smell it but managed to distant himself by thinking of the life he had left behind: the sun-drenched meadows of Hill Farm; Old Jack, Jezebel and Stanley, and the farm itself – the home he knew so well.

"I mustn't forget," he told himself. "I mustn't."

He drifted off to sleep and tried to remain that way for the rest of his journey. The voice in the darkness had been right. What good would knowing where he was going do? He would still not be able to control it.

Tom's cage was thrown down into thick mud with a *plop*. He awoke immediately.

"What have they sent us then?" A bawdy voice cried out. "A runt by the looks of it!"

Laughter followed, many deep voices at once, and Tom looked around at his surroundings.

Mud was everywhere. Under him, above him, lining the walls. The walls themselves seemed to be made from slats of wood, topped with bags of sand. The roof? There was none. Just a blue sky spotted with whisps of cloud.

The men surrounded him. Each wore a dark green coat, their heads covered with helmets. Hanging from their shoulders was a long weapon which reminded Tom of the shotgun that Old Jack used to keep hanging high on the wall in his farmhouse.

All in all, the men reminded Tom of the man on horseback who had come to Hill Farm to take him away. *Soldiers,* he thought. *Fighters. Like me. Mum always said I was a fighter.*

"Oi runt!" said the man again. He had a missing front tooth and spectacles. "You meant to be our mouser then?"

"Leave him be, Downes," said another man. He had a thin moustache which made him look somehow like he was in charge. "He's just scared. Give him some room."

The moustached man took the cage and gently unhooked the lock. He slowly opened the door and stood back. Tom, wary, stayed where he was.

"See, Sarge? They've sent us a dud," Downes laughed.

"Give him time. I'd stay put too if the first thing I saw was your ugly mug, Downes," said a large man stood by the wall.

"Bog off, Butler!" said Downes. "Not my fault if they sent us a coward."

Tom heard the word and stood up straight away.

"I am *not* a coward!" he said to himself. He walked out and held his head up high. The men cheered and Sarge held out his hand for Tom to sniff. It was a gesture of friendship that Tom recognised, so he sniffed the hand and rubbed his head against it. He explored his surroundings. The mud was a brown-grey colour he hadn't seen before; back in Devon the fields had been a glorious red. His surroundings seemed to be dug into the ground, like a rabbit burrow he had once come across.

If this is a rabbit burrow, it's huge! thought Tom. *No wonder Old Jack was always trying to shoot them with his shotgun.*

He walked his way around the trench, as the soldiers seemed to call it, and the men seemed to take a shine to him. Each stroked him, including the giant Butler. Downes continued to be rude.

"He's tiny though! How's he going to be of any use?" he said, sneering. Downes turned back to his mess tin, where he was about to tuck into some lunch.

Then Tom saw it – a small brown mouse perched on the lip of Downes's mess tin. His hunting instinct took over.

Lock eyes, sink low, wiggle bum, POUNCE!

He propelled himself forward towards Downes who, when he saw Tom with fangs bared and claws out leaping towards him, screamed.

"Eeeeeeeeeeeee!"

Tom landed with precision and swiped his paw down on the mouse, killing it in one go. The men applauded Tom and laughed at Downes, who sat with a frown while Tom looked on.

"Who's the coward *now*, Downesy?" said Butler. "He's only a kitten!"

Sarge took the mouse from Tom and slung it over the top of the trench, past the barb wire that circled the top.

"Good job, little 'un" he said to Tom. "And welcome to the trenches."

*

Tom stayed with the men for a while. They were nice people; they stroked and tickled him, laughed and cheered as he leapt long distances. He was hungry and sniffed around their mess tins until they caved in and gave him a scrap of food.

"Here, this'll be the test of him," called Butler. He stabbed a can opener into a can and cut off the lid. He offered it to Tom who approached it with care. He sniffed.

Mmm, meat! He thought. He licked it. It tasted salty, but delicious.

"Blimey, a cat with a taste for bully beef," said Sarge. "You won't go hungry then. Although if I were you, I'd stick to the mice.

An officer in his peaked cap came around the corner and the men dispersed.

"Don't give 'em a smidgen!" he barked. "The cats need to stay hungry. Keeps 'em hunting."

The soldiers busied themselves with cleaning their rifles and polishing their boots, but Tom was sure he saw Sarge give him a smile and a wink.

Tom, without the soldiers to entertain, started to prowl around. The trench was unlike any place he had been before. It was deep and narrow, with roads and alleys that confused him. He stayed around the area he had been delivered to, where the men lived and cooked. It seemed pleasant, but his instinct told him that behind their smiles, the men were unhappy, nervous and afraid.

"Maybe I could be of use here," Tom said to himself. "Hunt the mice, play with the soldiers."

It was nice to see the men smile. They did not do it often, especially if the officer was about.

Yes, thought Tom. *Maybe this new life won't be so bad after all.*

"HSSSSK!"

The blood-curdling hiss came from above Tom. Looking up he saw, on top of the sandbagged wall and next to the sharp barbed wire, a beast of a cat. He was black all over with matted fur and deep green eyes. He looked down at Tom and spat once more, baring his teeth, before leaping over the barbed wire and off into the land outside the trenches.

Chapter Five

Finding Friends

Tom soon learned that life in the trenches was hard. The men were friendly and welcoming at first, but later they were nervous and shouted a lot. The language that came from them used a lot of words that Tom had only heard once when Old Jack had accidentally hit his thumb with a hammer. Soon Tom discovered a new danger and the reason the men were nervous; fighting. When Tom had imagined the soldiers doing their job he had somehow thought that they would fight like he or Stanley would have fought on the farm, using their cunning, claws and teeth to defeat the rodents. But the men used their loud firesticks.

Tom was used to gunfire. Old Jack has used his shotgun to hunt rabbits or shoot pheasants in hunting season. Tom had jumped when he first heard the gun back on the farm, but he soon learned that it meant that he and Jezebel would have scraps of rabbit for tea. He would eventually start to salivate with hunger when he heard the distant pop-pop of a shotgun.

But nothing could prepare him for the shelling.

The sound was the worst part. From far away Tom's keen ears could pick up the bang of the enemy's gun as it fired. Next was the whistle as the shell sailed through the air. Tom would learn to hate that sound as it meant that fire and chaos was about to come. Then the shell landed. If it landed far away the sound was the only thing to fear. If it landed close by, Tom found that he and the soldiers would be splattered with mud. If it hit the trenches, that was when the screaming started and the calls of *'Medic!'* echoed around the dark dugout.

All this Tom would learn over time but on his first evening in the trenches he did as his mother had told him. He followed his instinct and *ran*.

The shell came down nearby. It rocked the trench and sent mud raining down on them. The men ducked and held on to their steel helmets, holding their position, but Tom was scared. He ran, sprinting as fast as his furry little legs could manage. He dashed from the main trench to the living quarters, where he sped and leapt onto a bunk in the darkest corner. There he pressed himself against the cold wall; shivering, alone, afraid.

"First night?"

The voice came from the darkness at the far end of the bunk. It was calm and soft, not frightened and shaky like Tom's.

"Wh-who's there?" he called. The darkness suddenly moved and Tom saw two emerald eyes shining back at him.

"At ease, soldier," said the voice. "I come in peace."

The voice was smooth, like butter on a warm summer's day. It reminded Tom of the comfort he felt when Jezebel would lick his fur clean. From out of the shadows, a white face and pointed ears emerged.

"Hello," said Tom. He felt breathless. He had never seen such a beautiful cat in all his life.

"Hello my sweet," said the white cat. "I'm Mary. What's your name then?"

"T-tom."

"Pleased to meet you T-tom," she joked. She paused and noticed a speck of mud on her front paw. She immediately licked it clean. "Although you'll have your name changed five time before sunrise, trust me. Soldiers have a knack for nick-names. First night?"

A mortar sailed above their heads and landed with a thud in the mud nearby. The bang shook the dugout and dust fell from the rafters. Tom crouched low, while Mary barely flinched. He rose, shaking.

"Never mind, my sweet," said Mary, ap-proaching him. She sniffed his head and Tom felt the tickle of her whiskers against his. "Hard to be-lieve it now but in a day or two you won't even no-tice them."

Mary was all white and older than Tom by a few years. He marvelled at the way she kept herself clean in the mud of the trenches. He had found it hard enough back home on the farm.

"I was shipped in today. I don't even know where I am," he said.

"Why, you're in France my dear!" said Mary with a laugh.

"France?" said Tom, turning over the word in his mind. "Is that near Hill Farm?"

Mary looked confused.

"I don't expect so…" A flare went up outside above them, lighting the trench up like it was noon. A shaft of light came in from the doorway. "Here my love, let's take a better look at you."

She hopped down to the ground and into the light, nodding to Tom to do the same. Once in position, she looked directly at him and laughed. "Why, you're just a kitten!"

Tom curled his lip in disgust.

"Am not! I can hunt! I've caught dozens of mice back at Hill Farm," he said. He puffed up his chest and sat up tall, attempting (and yet failing) to look grown up.

"Calm down my dear, no one said you didn't. I'm sure you're an excellent mouser."

"Hmph!"

The sound came from the dugout, where an officer's desk stood covered in papers and dust from the shelling. At the end of the desk sat a huge black and white cat with a tear on his left ear. He was so fat that Tom couldn't believe he hadn't noticed him when he came in.

"Something to say, Nelson?" said Mary loudly, like a teacher talking to a naughty child. Then, more softly to Tom: "That's Nelson. He thinks he's in charge around here."

Nelson sat up and turned towards Tom on the ground, looking down on him.

"It's not the mice that are the problem around here, boy," he said, his voice deep and trembling with age. "It's the rats."

Tom froze.

"Rats?"

He immediately thought of his encounter in the barn back at the farm. Those teeth...those red eyes...and how Stanley had limped and bled after defeating it.

"I...I don't like rats," he mumbled.

"Hmm? What's that? Speak up!" Nelson demanded.

"I don't like rats," Tom repeated. He had shrunk back into the shadows.

"Like? Like? There is nothing to *like* about rats, boy! You'll have to do your job properly or not at all."

Mary tutted.

"Go easy on the lad, Nelson. It's his first night," she said. She stood closer to Tom to show her support for him. "You'll have to excuse him, Tom. He's been in service his whole life. He forgets some of us weren't born into it."

"Nonsense! Don't mollycoddle the boy, Mary," said Nelson. He stood and leapt down to the floor with more grace than Tom would have thought was possible for a cat his size. He walked straight up to Tom and looked him in the eye, challenging him. "You're in the army now, sonny."

"But...I never asked to be!" Tom said. He heard the childish whine in his voice and instantly regretted it. Nelson laughed.

"Ha! Do you think those men out there asked to be here? To leave their loved ones? To sit in the cold mud and shoot at strangers all day?" he sneered. "Do your bit. Like it or lump it."

Nelson resumed his position on the officer's desk and Mary led Tom back to the bunk where they spent the night. Tom counted himself lucky that he had met someone as warm and kind as her. He thought about Nelson too. He seemed bullish and unsympathetic, but something told Tom that it came from a good place; like Stanley back on the farm, he was firm and sometimes mean, but Tom knew that he meant well. He also knew that Nelson was right. He didn't like ratting, but he was stuck there now and had to make the best of it. However scared he was of rats, he knew that he could never be as scared as the men in the trenches. Just as he was about to drift off to sleep, the image of the dirty black cat with the deep green eyes came back into his mind.

"Mary?"

"Hmm?" said Mary dozily. "What is it Tom?"

"I saw another cat today. He was all black and hissed at me."

"That'll be The Kaiser," she said. "At least that's what the soldiers call him. After some king or some such. He might as well be, around here. King, that is. Rumour has it he was feral once. He can take down a rat in seconds."

Tom thought for a while.

"Does he sleep here too?" he asked. The prospect frightened him a little.

"No, he works for the other side," said Mary.

"Other side?"

"The enemy, boy!" came Nelson's deep growl from across the dugout. "Them what the soldiers are fighting, He's a *German*. Now, go to sleep."

Tom was silent now. The black cat – The Kaiser – had come all the way across the bomb ridden landscape between the two fronts from the enemy side. Tom had barely even known there *was* an enemy.

"Mary?"

"What, Tom?" she muttered, getting irritated now.

"Why did he hiss at me?" he asked. "Does he hate me?"

"Don't worry, my sweet," said Mary. She closed her eyes and lay her chin on her paws, trying once more to get to sleep. "It's The Kaiser. He hates *everybody*."

Chapter Six

Off to the Front

Tom settled in. Mary was a good friend and helped him find his way around.

"When you're begging for scraps, never go to an officer. They get the best food but they're the least likely to give you any," she would tell him. "Go for the skinny ones. The Privates are more generous. Give 'em a purr and they'll melt like butter."

"How do I know which ones they are?" asked Tom.

"They'll be eating from their mess tins," said Mary. "The ones looking sad and lost."

Tom peeked out of the corner of the dugout he had taken as his own. A man in uniform wearing a steel helmet stood just outside the door of the dugout and stared into space. His face was young but almost grey with fear, exhaustion and worry.

"Why are they so sad?" said Tom. He had seen plenty of those pitiful, empty expressions in the short time he had lived in the trenches.

"You forget, Thomas," said Nelson, still in his permanent position of weighing down the papers on the officer's desk. "Many of these men have been torn from their homes too. Some have only just left school and then they were shipped over to this hell-hole and told to do..." He paused. "...*dreadful* things."

Tom looked at the private once more and saw that he was lonely as well as scared.

"We should comfort them," said Tom under his breath. Nelson laughed.

"Your job is to kill vermin, Young Thomas," he said. "Nothing more, nothing less."

"Don't call me that! My name's Tom! But anyway, if we-"

"But nothing!" shouted Nelson. "You do your job or you ship off back to Blighty."

He harrumphed and leapt down from the desk with a thud. He walked out into the breach.

"Wh-what did I say?" asked Tom. Mary soothed him with a purr.

"Don't you worry about it my sweet," she said. "Like I said before, Nelson has been in service

47

a long time. He's seen such a lot of action. Not all scars can be seen from the outside, you know."

Tom didn't really understand, but he stayed quiet from then on around Nelson. He constantly thought about why they were there, stuck in a hole in the muddiest place on Earth.

Until now Tom had remained in the reserve trench, where the soldiers ate and slept. He hadn't seen much fighting to speak of, apart from the shelling and an argument between two men over a magazine with the picture of a pretty woman in it. When he had found he would be with soldiers, he expected fighting and heroics, but he had seen more cups of tea than he had seen bullets.

"If this is a war," he wondered aloud one day to a still-grumpy Nelson and the forever flawless Mary. "Where is the fighting? I want to bare my claws and sink my teeth into the enemy...whoever they are..."

Nelson grunted a response."The fire trench. It's not a place of glamour, Thomas – I mean *Tom* – but it'll toughen you up quick enough."

"Pipe down Nelson!" said Mary. "You'll be putting ideas into his head. The front line is no place for a kitten."

"I'm not a kitten!" Tom protested, but neither cat was listening.

"It exactly what he needs," said Nelson. "He's hid back here for too long. It's time he saw what these men are doing here."

"He could get hurt!"

"He'll be fine. He's young and fast."

"Faster than a bullet?" said Mary.

Tom rolled his eyes as they discussed him like he wasn't there. He stood and left while they were still bickering.

He trotted out of the doorway, through the make-shift curtain and out into the open air. He found himself surrounded by sandbags once more and made his way down the narrow corridors of mud, over the planks of wood which were intended to provide some stability over the slushy soil at the base of the trench. He walked down the support trench where nervous soldiers waited for orders to march to the front. They smoked, cleaned their guns and read the army newspapers while they waited, or simply slept in their funkhole, a small makeshift cubbyhole in which the Privates managed to get some shut-eye.

Tom marvelled at how many people there were. In the reserve trench he had seen people come and go, but he had never seen them all at once. He wondered if the reserve trenches were safer too, as that was where he got the most attention. Here in the support trench he got no strokes or scraps of food – the men clearly had other things on their minds.

Tom walked and walked, stopping only to drink from a puddle and pick off a cheeky mouse or two. The trenches were not in a straight line as he had expected (it felt like he was walking down rows of corn back on Hill Farm), but zigzagged along so that he was constantly turning corners and soon felt quite lost.

His nose twitched and he was bowled over by a horrid smell as he turned a corner. Nelson's warning echoed back in his mind:

It's not a place of glamour, Thomas…

Smoke hung in the air. It was the familiar smell of burning gunpowder that reminded Tom of Old Jack's shotgun in hunting season. There was another smell mixing with it: the stench of manure and urine which came from an open latrine several hundred yards away. Tom found himself wishing he didn't have such a sensitive sense of smell.

"So this is the fire trench," Tom said to himself. He couldn't help but be disappointed. He had envisioned a cosy hearth and a large rocking chair like Jack's fireside at Hill Farm.

The wall was the usual sandbag and mud arrangement with an occasional parapet through which a soldier could position their rifle. Along the base of the wall was a large concrete step. A few men would stand on it and poke their head above the wall, looking for enemy on the other side. Others used an ingenious device made of mirrors to peek over the top.

The step was also used, Tom was glad to learn, as a place to sleep. He had walked a fair few miles from the reserve trench without so much as a scrap of food, so was long overdue a nap.

He would usually curl up on an officer's bunk or find a secluded corner to kip in, but there was no such comfort here. He jumped up to the concrete step where two of the soldiers were asleep, catching forty winks while they could.

Tom desperately wanted some form of warmth and so climbed carefully onto the chest of the nearest soldier.

"Sorry!" said Tom to the Private, but he was so light that the soldier did not even stir. Tom padded down the area of his chest he had chosen as a bed and lay down. A light purr emanated from him as he drifted off to sleep...

Chapter Seven

A Close Shave

The soldier woke with a start, as if coming around from a dream of bad memories. As soon as he awoke he realised that he should have stayed dreaming – he was already in a nightmare.

Tom awoke too but had only been dozing peacefully, a light slumber where he had dreamt of chasing butterflies on Hill Farm. Dreams and reality had started to blend until he finally woke, confused.

"What the-?" the soldier began. He was confused to see the furry ginger face in front of him, just inches from his nose. "Hullo? How long have you been there?"

Tom could only reply with a purr. It was warm on the boy's chest and surprisingly comfortable. It was definitely a boy; the soldier smelled of aftershave, presumably applied to cover the stench of his uniform or to block the smell of the latrines, as he had no beard growth to speak of. Tom had seen enough soldiers to know that they either had moustaches (the officers) or a day's growth of stubble and this one had neither. He was little more than a child but that was okay, Tom decided – some people even still mistook him for a kitten, although he was nearly eight months old.

"Oi Sanders!" called another soldier. "Who's yer twin?"

This confused both Tom and the soldier for a second until he smiled and sat up. Tom leapt off his chest. He removed his helmet to show a shock of bright ginger hair.

"Wow, like me!" said Tom. The other men laughed and jeered.

"It's ginger Jim and a ginger Tom!" they called. Jim, the red headed Private, took the ribbing with a laugh and a smile.

"They're harmless," he said to Tom, rubbing his head playfully. It's the ones on the other side you've got to beware of." He nodded to the top of the wall, past the barbed wire.

Tom still hadn't had enough sleep so he jumped back onto Jim's lap. Jim stroked him fondly.

"I hate to break up the romance Sanders, but last time I checked this was a war," said a captain. "Now stand-to!"

Tom felt Jim's hesitation but within seconds he was on his feet and up on the concrete plinth, or 'fire step' as the soldiers seemed to call it. Jim readied his rifle but stopped and looked around.

"What are you waiting for boy?" barked the captain. The assembled soldiers sniggered until one private stepped forward with an old apple crate.

"Here y'go Jim," he said. "Give 'em hell."

Jim blushed and took the crate. He placed it down on the fire step and stepped on it so he could reach the top of the wall. The captain shook his head in disbelief and walked off, barking orders at others. Tom looked up at Jim with the same questioning look that the captain had used.

"What?" said Jim with a grin. "You're no giant yourself!"

Tom settled down to rest on a discarded knapsack while Jim poked the end of his rifle through the sandbagged parapet. He prepared himself to aim and fire, but it meant putting his head above the wall and staring out into the muddy wasteland between the two front lines – and straight into the sights of the enemy. Tom picked up on his nervousness; the sweating brow, the shaking hand. It was like his nerves were vibrating through Tom, like their bodies had synchronised in that short time they had spent sleeping.

"Good job, Jimbo!" said the private who had handed him the crate. "Great way to impress the top brass!"

"Get knotted Biggsy!" laughed Jim. "Here, pass us that ammo, will ya?"

Biggsy, a tall brute of a man with a rain cape and steel helmet, grabbed a box of bullets and stepped up to the fire step, where he was taller than Jim, even with the apple crate.

Then Tom felt it.

It was a feeling he knew well, but he did not know why he was experiencing it *now*.

It was *instinct*.

The same immediate fear he had felt when he first encountered the giant rat in the barn. He looked around and saw no rats but when he looked up at Jim, the feeling struck him all the more.

TRUST YOUR INSTINCTS!

Jezebel's final words to him rang out in his mind and he knew what he had to do.

He leapt out at Jim, reaching up to him and grabbing hold of his leg. He dug his claws into Jim's thigh so the boy screamed out in pain.

"Agh! Get 'im off me!" he yelled. Biggsy laughed as Jim fell from his apple crate into the mud below. Jim was prying Tom from his leg when-

Tat! Ratatatatatat!

Biggsy's laugh stopped and he fell to the ground, clutching his head. Jim threw Tom across the trench and went to help his friend, Tom landing safely on all four paws.

"Biggsy! You all right?" yelled Jim. Biggsy moaned and turned to Jim. He moved his hand to reveal his injury. There was no blood, as Jim had been expecting, but his steel helmet had a bullet hole through the rim. Jim removed it and gulped.

"That was a close one!" he said, staring in amazement at the damaged helmet.

"I'll say," said Biggsy. "That cat. He...he...he *saved* you."

Jim looked over to where Tom sat, patiently cleaning his paw.

"You're welcome," said Tom. He walked up and rubbed his head against Jim's leg. "Sorry about the scratches. Couldn't think how else to get your attention."

Tom was astounded at how strong the instinct had been. He hadn't known what was coming, just that something *bad* was about to happen. The moment he looked at Jim, he knew he had to save him. He had trusted his instincts and it had probably saved Jim's life. Had he been indecisive, he would have certainly been too late. The whole episode had taken less than a second.

Biggsy went off to get a new helmet and a stiff drink, while Jim sat and cleaned the mud off his rifle. Tom sat next to him all the while.

"You saved me," Jim muttered, still not quite believing it. Tom purred.

"I suppose I did," he said modestly.

Jim spied the aluminium disc on Tom's collar.

"Hullo? What we got here then?" He reached out to take a closer look. "That's an ID tag. Same as mine, look."

Jim reached under his shirt and pulled out his small round disc which was the only way of identifying him. His was a worn red colour, made of a different material but still emblazoned with his name, religion and regiment. He tickled Tom and looked at his tag.

T.J. HILL

C OF E

1st DEVONS REGT

Tom purred at the tickles but was confused over Jim's fascination with the thing around his neck. Old Jack had put it there the day he had left Hill Farm, but Tom had never even seen it. It was out of his line of sight and anyway, he was a cat – he couldn't even *read* the stupid thing.

"Hill, eh?" said Jim. Tom looked up at the mention of his old home. "TJ? What's that stand for? Timmy?"

"Oh, please!" said Tom.

"Terrance?" Jim said. Another withering look came from Tom. "Got it. Tom! You *are* a ginger tom after all! And a Devonshire lad!"

Tom had no idea what Jim was saying but nuzzled his fist anyway. It was nearing lunchtime and Tom was certain that Jim had some bully beef somewhere on him.

"The 1st Devonshire Regiment..." Jim continued. "They recruited from Bow, didn't they? That's my neck of the woods. Just a few miles over the hill in Tawton, that's my Da's farm. We're neighbours!"

The officer came around the corner and Jim jumped back on duty. He took one look down at Tom before stepping up to look through the rifle's sights.

"Is it safe?" he asked the kitten.

Tom thought for a moment. No tingles. No danger.

"Yes!" he mewed and the young soldier went back to his duty.

After a long shift another Private, caked in mud, arrived and tapped Jim on the shoulder.

"All change!" he said. "Quiet?"

"Just a cheeky beggar to the east there," he replied. "Occasionally he lets off a round, but then retreats back. I think he's a coward, truth be told."

"What about this one?" the private pointed down to Tom, who was curled up on the fire step in a ball.

"He's with me," said Jim, winking. "My lucky charm."

He whistled through his teeth, the way he always had done when summoning the cats on his father's farm. Tom woke, stretched, and followed Jim out of the fire trench like an obedient sheep dog. They turned back up to the support trench with Tom trotting behind, to the amazement and joy of all those around.

Jim didn't even strip off his outer layer of waterproofs before sitting down for a rest. He found a funkhole and sat, his limbs aching, his eyes closing.

His tired, blurry vision recognised the orange shape in front of him and Jim gave his whistle from his teeth.

Tom leapt up.

"About time!" Tom muttered. "Hang on, stay still. I've got an idea."

Tom jumped from Jim's lap to his shoulder, where he crept around his neck and lay like a pillow across his shoulders. Jim pulled his hood up and lay back gently so he was resting on Tom, his tail curling down his front like a neck tie.

"How'd you end up here, little Tom?" he muttered. Sleep was trying to claim him but the gunshots in the trenches kept him awake. "Like all of us, I expect? You were promised an adventure, but given a hell."

Tom purred, although truthfully the only adventure he ever wanted was to be the best mouser on the farm.

Back home, I was fresh out of school when I signed up. I had worked on my Da's farm, but I only wanted to get out of Devon and see the world," Jim said drowsily. "Funny that. Now all I want to do is see those red rolling hills again. And Daisy of course."

Tom let out a questioning mew, as if to say '*who?*'.

"She lived on the farm a few fields over. Neighbours, we was. Known her since I was in nappies. She was my sweetheart, I suppose you'd say."

Tom began to trail off into a slumber, his new friend's voice acting like warm milk on a winter's night.

"But I had to go and argue with my Da, didn't I? He didn't want me to enlist. I said it was my duty. We had a blazing row and I went down to Tawton the next day. I was too young of course. Looked it, too. I told the officer I was eighteen. He looked me up and down and told me to come back the next day and see if I was nineteen. Then they gave me a rifle and here I am."

The gunfire was getting heavier and Tom could feel Jim's heart beat faster. He purred long and loud and the heart rate dropped.

"The war can't last forever, Tom," said Jim. "I'll make you a deal. You keep me safe like you did today. Get me through the war and I'll get us back to Devon. I'll say sorry to Da and get Daisy to marry me. You can catch mice and sit by the fire. How's that sound?"

But the only response from Tom was the gentle movement of his chest as he slept soundly, purring into the night...

Chapter Eight

Life in Battle

Life on the front line wasn't all naps and snack times, as Tom soon learned. While Jim liked having him around, the officers in charge would shoo him away, so Tom found it best to let Jim get on with his duties. Tom, of course, had his own duties.

The mice in the trenches were tough. Not only did they put up with the constant shots from the guns and the barrage of fire from the enemy, but they had to put up with the food as well. A soldier's rations were not much to sniff at, as Tom had found. He enjoyed the bully beef and sometimes some scraps of grey-coloured meat that the privates fished out of a pie, but otherwise he did as the captain had suggested and stuck to eating the mice.

And there were hundreds. Maybe even thousands of them, crawling through the mud of the trenches and burrowing into the dugouts. Tom's best trick was just to wait by the supplies and pounce on the mice as they poked their heads out.

He had started to take them as presents to the soldiers but no one seemed to appreciate them, so instead he took them as snacks for himself.

The rest of the time he would spend with Jim. Tom would come to see him once they had both finished their duties for the day. Jim would relax into his funkhole and Tom would join him, purring and providing comfort.

"Are you two married or what?" joked Biggsy.

"Just good mates," said Jim.

There were days when Jim would play with him and stroke him from head to tail, and others when he would come off the fire step and just sit and stare. Tom would sit by him to soothe him, but got the impression that he was lost in his own thoughts.

"Sorry, Tom," Jim would say. "Sometimes you see things around here...you see things you can't un-see. Stuff I wouldn't wish on my worst enemy."

And Tom knew what he meant.

One night, as Jim was asleep in his funkhole, Tom got up to stretch. It was pitch black in the trenches but the sky was suddenly lit up by the flash from artillery fire. Each army used huge guns that could launch explosives at each other and one had landed just a hundred yards away. Tom felt the rush of heat as the sky lit up and he leapt back.

The trenches were built in a zig-zag pattern so that a fire would not sweep down and destroy everything they had built and Tom knew that he was safe. He also knew that many of Jim's friends would have been lost in the blast.

*

There was more to contend with in the trenches than just the enemy. There were pests of all kinds; rats, mice and flies were drawn by the stink of the latrines and the smell of dead bodies. Lice would crawl over the men and leave them itching like a dog. Disease was rife too, but Jim thankfully remained healthy. And then there was the weather.

"I ain't seen rain like this since I had an holiday in Bognor!" shouted Biggsy. The rain came down in buckets while the soldiers were on hand to bail out the trenches. Jim worked fast, scooping up water and pouring it away into a channel that took it away from their quarters. The storm had not stopped for hours and Tom had taken refuge at the first sign of rain.

He found his way back to the officer's bunks, having hitched a ride on a barrow that was being used to transport a wounded man.

"Well, well, well!" said a familiar voice. "Thomas, as I live and breathe!"

"Hello Nelson," said Tom. He walked over to the stove which was burning nicely and fell to the floor. He was exhausted and wet.

"Tom!" Mary ran to him and started to lick him clean. "Where have you been? We've- well, *I've* been worried sick!" Tom laughed and pushed her away.

"I've missed you too! Now stop fussing!"

Nelson let out a short 'Ha!'.

"What are you laughing about, you old fleabag?" snapped Mary. "The boy was gone for weeks. He could have been killed!"

Nelson sat up on his desk and gave Tom what looked to be a bow.

"I recognise that attitude!" he said. "You've been to the front line, haven't you?"

Mary gasped and looked to Tom to see if it was true. Tom didn't meet her gaze.

"Tom! You...you..."

"Could have been killed? Yes, but I wasn't. I was safe," Tom said. He licked his muddy front paw clean.

"Safe? There's no such thing around here! The men put us in danger the moment they dumped us here!"

Nelson rolled his eyes at Mary.

"Oh, do be quiet!" he said. "I want to hear what it's like at the front! Tell us, boy!"Tom paused. He knew what Nelson wanted to hear. He had been born into service and had lived through countless battles. He wanted to hear about the fighting, the casualties, the victories. But Tom did not want to dwell on it.

"Plenty of mice," he muttered. Nelson lay back down, disappointed.

"And the men?" said Mary, fussing around him. "Were they kind? Did they give you scraps?"

Tom's mood lightened at the thought of Jim and his kindness.

"Yeah, they're fun. There's this one boy, Jim. He's really nice to me and he's said that when he gets through this, he's going to take me back to Devon with him."

Mary's look changed. She somehow looked more worried.

"Oh. That's...nice, Tom."

From the desk came a low chortle, which slowly turned into a deep laugh.

"What's so funny, Nelson?" Tom asked.

"My dear boy," Nelson began. "I was once like you. Young, nimble and naïve. I started on the ships, you know. The ship's cat on the HMS Dreadnought. Not many rats, but lots of mice and of course a bunch of sailors. I was their good luck charm. It was them who named me of course. I'd let them stroke me and feed me and they said they'd take me ashore so I could retire. Every time we docked in Plymouth it was the same story. They'd disembark, move on, and I'd never see them again."

The dugout was silent for a moment, apart from the hammering rain on the roof. This time it was Mary who could not meet Tom's eye.

"No, Jim's not like that. He's...different," Tom protested. "He lived not far from Hill Farm and he'll take me back there once-"

"Thomas, people come and go, never thinking for a moment about the likes of us. You're at war now. Do you think they're going to transport strays like us back across to Blighty?" said Nelson. Tom wanted to protest again, but a shiver went down his spine. It wasn't instinct this time, but a horrific realisation that Nelson might be right. "We're stuck here. You'll never see Hill Farm again and no one will save you. The sooner you realise that, the better."

*

Tom had hidden away under a bunk for the rest of the night and emerged only at the first sign of dawn. He didn't want to see Nelson or Mary and so crept out of the dugout into the reserve trench and the bright light of the sunrise.

The day looked to be a good one after the previous night's storm and Tom spent the first half hour sat on top of a damp sandbag on a wall, just lazing in the sun.

The troops were fairly quiet at that time and Tom seemed to be the only one who noticed a bird flutter down onto the wall.

"Mornin' squire!" said the tubby pigeon.

"Um...good morning," muttered Tom. He wasn't used to having birds talk to him, unless it was the cheeky old crows back on Hill Farm. He noticed the pigeon had something attached around his leg.

"Who's in charge here?" the pigeon asked. "I normally get a handful of feed if I make it here in one piece. It's no joke, I tell you, flying all the way from HQ with this thing on your leg. Throws your balance right off, it does."

Tom was confused at the pigeon, talking as though he was a soldier.

"What's that?" Tom asked, nodding to the ring on his foot.

"Message for the men. That's my job – flying forwards and backwards, delivering messages," he said.

"What does it say?"

"How should I know? I'm a pigeon!" he said. "Orders for the troops usually."

Tom's mind began to race.

"Maybe it's good news? Maybe the war is over!"

The pigeon spotted its feeding loft nearby and prepared for take off.

"I hate to break it to you, furrball," he said with a ruffle of feathers. "But it's never *good* news."

Chapter Nine

A Message from Afar

Tom walked the few miles through soggy mud to the fire trench. It took him most of the day and by the time he had reached the men, they were sullen and silent.

"So the featherhead was right," Tom muttered to himself. "It wasn't good news."

He prowled among the soldiers, rubbing past their legs and trying to get a tickle or a stroke, but none responded. He saw Jim sat on the fire step and trotted up to him, mewing a welcome.

"Hello Tom," Jim said, without feeling. Tom noticed his mood and leapt onto his lap. Jim reluctantly stroked him.

What's up? You've got a face longer than a cart horse's," said Tom. All Jim heard was a small mew.

"Tonight's the night," whispered Jim, almost to himself rather than Tom. "We're going over..."

Tom froze.

He knew what that meant. Many men in the trench had spoken of going 'over the top' and had talked about it with some sense of expectation and glee. They were like coiled springs, ready to leap over the barbed wire and charge at the enemy, walking slowly so as not to fall. As Tom looked around, he saw some of the same men who had expressed disappointment that they weren't getting any 'action', but now they had the order to attack they looked grey with worry.

"All right lads, stop your moping," said the Captain. He stood up and puffed his chest out, trying to look brave.

"You don't fool me," muttered Tom to himself. "You're as scared as the rest of them. Cats can sense these things, y'know."

"We go over the top at dawn. Use this time to clean your weapons, check your ammo, eat and – if you can – sleep."

The soldiers laughed. There was no way any of them were sleeping tonight.

While Biggsy took the lookout, Jim retreated to a funkhole and drank steaming hot tea from a chipped enamel cup. With Tom flopped around his neck like a fox-fur, he reached into his pocket and pulled out a wad of paper, tied in a red ribbon. Tom's sensitive nose could make out a number of scents on the paper; rosewater, ink and apples.

Smells like home, he thought. *Like Devon.*

Jim looked through the papers one by one. Luckily there was no rain that night for the first time since he could remember, so the paper didn't get wet.

"This is Daisy," said Jim. Tom remembered the name: Jim's sweetheart from his home. "She writes everyday. I only get them in dribs and drabs when the post gets through but I keep every one. I dunno what she finds to write about," he laughed.

"Does it matter?" said Tom, purring in Jim's ear. "As long as she's thinking of you." He could tell what the letters meant to him. He kept every piece of paper clean and crisp, dry and tucked up tight with its neighbour, sealed in its bow.

"We'll get home, Tom," Jim slurred. He was falling asleep, the warm body of Tom acting like a feather pillow. "We'll get home somehow."

As the boy fell into dreamland, his weight pressing pleasingly on Tom's body, Tom felt the rarest thing; he was close to Jim, not just in body, but in spirit. He had found a true friend and soul mate, one that had sworn to take him home and would, Tom believed, follow through on his promise.

Jim snored, and Tom began to drift too. As he closed his eyes, he made a silent pact with himself.

I will never leave you, he thought. *You are my friend and my ticket out of here. Besides, I'm your good luck charm. You won't stand a chance without me.*

Chapter Ten

Awaiting the Whistle

"Look alive, boyo!" came the barking voice of Jim's Commanding Officer. "We've got Gerry to thrash!"

Jim groaned but stood up immediately, his basic training coming into action. He blinked a few times and was ready for action, apart from the cat around his neck.

"Oi! Gerrof!" he said. Tom woke suddenly from a blissful dream; he had been back at Hill Farm and Old Jack was treating him to the cream from the dairy. He stood and leapt from Jim's shoulders, who luckily wasn't very tall so Tom landed feet first on the ground.

"What? What's going on?" he said, looking about, confused. Then he remembered. It was time to go over the top.

Jim bent down and stroked Tom's head, who looked up at him with a quizzical expression.

"I'll be gone for a bit. You wait for me, yeah? I'll be back soon and then we're gonna figure out how to get back home. You be good while I'm gone."

"MEEEEEOOOOOWWW!" cried Tom as Jim pulled his rifle onto his shoulder. As Jim followed the procession of soldiers toward the fire trench, Tom trotted behind.

"What are you doing? Stay here, you daft moggy!" said Jim through his teeth, trying not to attract the attention of his C.O. "It's not safe. What do you think we're doing? Going for a prance in the meadow?"

"Of course it's not safe," said Tom. "That's why I'm coming. To keep *you* safe."

As Jim arrived in the fire trench, Tom was just a pace behind. Looking annoyed and petrified at the same time, Jim waited until his C.O's back was turned, then bent down and picked up Tom.

"You stay here. D'y'hear?" he said. He held him by the scruff of the neck, which didn't hurt Tom. What did hurt him however was the look of terror and anger in Jim's eyes. "One of us has to be safe. Looks like that's you." He held Tom up so that their eyes met, their ginger hair mirroring each other. "GET IT?"

With that he threw Tom away onto the muddy ground where he landed on his paws, safe and unhurt. He could see that Jim meant it though. He could see that the words were not just said to show bravado to his friends. He wanted Tom to be safe. Which meant…

"He feels the same. Same as me," said Tom to himself. "We're soulmates."

The Officer barked his commands at the troops while they attached their bayonets to their rifles. Eighteen inches of polished Sheffield steel, with a point at the end that was as sharp as a razor. Jim, attaching it and marvelling at how deadly it looked, hoped to God that the Germans didn't have something similar.

"As per your training, you are to proceed on foot across no-man's-land. Walk in lines, at a steady pace. Those running will be be more likely to fall and become a sitting target for Gerry."

"Instead of a slow-moving target you mean?" said Biggsy under his breath. Jim, in spite of his terror, let out a snort of laughter.

"Keep your gas mask handy. There's no telling what Gerry will try and pull when we surprise 'em. If you see a gas attack coming, get your mask on quick and get it on right. If you don't you'll be a goner in no time," said the captain. "Gentlemen, good luck. The ladders, if you please". Soldiers carrying trench ladders appeared from behind Jim as if from nowhere and placed them against the sandbagged wall. "On my mark." The captain checked his watch and placed his tin whistle to his lips.

Tom looked on.

His heart was racing, fearing the worst for his friend. He longed to jump on him, to pull him back, but knew it would do no good. As the men prepared to climb the ladders and launch themselves into the sights of the enemy, a strange silence came over the trench.

The bombs, thought Tom. *They've stopped.*

"Artillery assault finished," said Biggsy. "Now it's our turn."

"Oh good," said Jim flatly. "Just march over and mop up the mess then?"

"That's the idea."

Eyes were on the captain's whistle. The men awaited their order.

"Gentlemen, attack!"

The whistle sounded and the soldiers leapt forward as if on springs. They mounted the ladders easily and from Tom's view of it all, most walked forwards out of sight. At least one fell forward after the first step into no-man's-land and did not get up again.

Jim did not glance back at Tom, as he hoped he might. He climbed the ladder automatically, heaving his heavy rifle which was taller than he was. Then he was gone. Out of sight.

Tom sat in the empty trench. He was hungry, but did not move to find mice. He was restless, but did not rise and run. He just wanted to wait for Jim to return.

"He'll be back. He'll be back."

Then a shiver ran down Tom's spine like a bolt of lightning. He had felt it a few times before and knew just what it meant.

Instinct.

The same as when he saw the rat in the barn. The same as when he pounced on Jim. Now...what? Where was the danger?

The sound of gunfire echoed over the trench wall, along with shouts and screams.

Tom knew what he had to do. Despite Jim's protests, he had to join him. He had to warn him of the danger. To guide him to safety.

Tom was going over the top.

Chapter Eleven

Over the Top

Tom leapt up the ladder like it was an apple tree back at Hill Farm and used his claws to grip onto the sandbags at the top. Heaving himself up, he heard a shout of a soldier from within the trench.

"Oi! Y' daft moggy! Get back here!"

But Tom ignored him. He only felt the electricity passing down his spine, telling him to move, and fast. His head peeked above the wall and he saw the carnage for the first time.

Mud, everywhere. It was what Tom had been expecting but the rest was alien to him. Barbed wire lay in front of him; coils and coils of sharp metal that would cut through a soldier's uniform in seconds. If you got caught then you'd stop on the spot and become the sitting target the C.O. had warned about. Tom looked to the side where other soldiers had mounted the ladders and saw two such soldiers that had caught their trousers on the wire. They had been shot where they stood, just yards from their own trench.

Jim, thought Tom. *I must find him.*

He ran out into the battlefield, leaping over clods of mud and stopped at the tangle of barbed wire.

"Easy," he said, trying to convince himself. "Just like a thicket of brambles back at the farm. Just take it slowly..."

Being small had its advantages. Tom eased his body into the wire at the widest point, keeping his head low and his tail even lower. He had to turn halfway through, bending his spine at an unnatural angle. He took his time over it, aware that he had to get to Jim fast, but also aware that he need to get there in one piece if he was to warn him of the danger he sensed.

"Nearly there..."

He poked his head out of the other side, extended his paw onto the mud and breathed a sigh of relief. He stepped out of the barbed wire, confident and cocky, until-

"Ow!"

His tail caught on a barb on the way out, trapping it. He pulled, a natural reaction, but the wrong one. His tail spiked with pain as his saw the ginger fur rip from his skin and a cut appear.

"Ah! Stupid, stupid, stupid!" he cursed himself. He had not allowed for the unruly tail on his bottom and now he was bleeding. It wasn't deep, and he licked it clean quickly, but it was a powerful - and painful – reminder that he should take extreme care.

No time to waste, he thought. *Find Jim*

He ran, the sound of guns and screams loud in his little ears. He was scared, in pain, but he imagined what Nelson would be saying to him if he were there.

You think those boys aren't scared? They're petrified. They want to go home. They want to see their families. But they can't. They are doing their duty and so should you.

"All right, all right," said Tom aloud. "I get the point, old man..."

Running at his full speed he saw soldiers up ahead. His friend had to be in there somewhere, but where?

"Why do they all have to wear the same colour clothes? I can't tell one from the other!"

The soldiers had fallen to the ground, taking cover behind a mound of earth. One was using his bayonet to dig himself further down, keeping his head down so as not to attract attention. Tom recognised two of them; it was Sarge and Butler, two of the first men he had met when he arrived in the trenches.

"This is a bleedin' mess, ay Sarge?" yelled Butler.

"True, Butler, true. We must play the hand we've been dealt though. Try to attack the enemy, even though they have superior firepower."

"And the advantage of being in their own trench? Surrounded by armour and ammo?"

Sarge winced.

"Yes. No one said it was a *perfect* plan..."

The two men took turns in firing shots to-wards the enemy line, risking their lives as they put their heads above the mound of earth. Tom trotted up to them and mewed.

"'Ello sunshine," said Butler. "Sorry, no snacks for you this time. I'm a bit busy."

"What the blazes is he doing here?" shouted Sarge above the hail of gunfire.

He tried to shoo Tom away with his foot, but Tom was stubborn and knew that he was safer with them.

"Suit yourself," said Sarge. He lifted his head to aim his rifle and fired -

Click.

"You out of ammo?" said Butler. Sarge nodded. "Well then, only one thing for it."

"Pineapples at the ready!"

The two men fumbled in their uniform and brought out two metal balls with pins in the top – hand grenades. They glanced at each other and ripped out the pins with their free hands.

"You may want to run away now..." said Butler to Tom. Tom didn't have time to work out what he was talking about before the two men rose from the ground and bowled the grenades towards the enemy lines like master cricketers.

BOOM!

Mud flew up from the German trench and sprayed far and wide. Tom finally did as Butler said and ran, while the two soldiers ran towards the enemy, bayonets raised and screaming at the top of their lungs.

Tom ran. He didn't know where he was or where he was going but the need to run outweighed the need to find out.

"This place...this is crazy!" he panted, out of breath. "They're killing each other!"

"What were you expecting?" came a voice from behind him. Tom stopped. "Card games and cocoa?"

Turning to the source of the voice, Tom was struck with fear.

The Kaiser.

He was as black at the night and blended in with a stump of a tree that had been blown up and burnt. Only his green eyes shone as a flare from an explosion far off lit them up.

"You've come quite far out of your way, little boy," said The Kaiser. He stood and walked slowly towards Tom. His voice was thin and sounded like nails scratching down a blackboard. "Very far indeed."

Tom remained still. Something about the cat scared him. Maybe it was his fearlessness. Cats could sense fright and The Kaiser had none. He was a beacon of calm amidst the chaos and killing.

"You were hunting, yes? Well, this is *my* land. You should turn back now. There are no rats for you here."

"Hunting? No I...I'm looking for my friend," Tom managed to say. He tried not to show fear also, but it was written on his face.

"A friend? Admirable, but..." he walked up to Tom, coming to within an inch of his face. "...you are looking in the WRONG PLACE." He spat the last words. Tom flinched but held his ground.

"H-have you seen him? He's small, ginger like me, and I need to tell him something..."

The Kaiser paused, then laughed.

"You want to tell the human something? Ah, that is priceless!" he smiled. "As though humans were capable of understanding us cats! My child, they do not have the brain power. They can not even fight their own wars in a reasonable manner. They cause devastation wherever they go."

"Why do you say that?"

The Kaiser backed away from Tom.

"Look around you. Is this the product of a reasonable animal?" he said. All around them was mud and fire. "Cats fight their own battles, isn't that right? We fight with teeth and claws. Men fight with fire and metal."

Tom moved to leave.

"Jim's not like that. He's my friend," he muttered as he turned to walk away. He heard the thudding of paws and then a great weight on his back as The Kaiser pounced on him. The black cat screamed and hissed as he pushed Tom to the ground. He opened his mouth to bite down on Tom's ear, but Tom was more flexible than the old cat and wriggled out of his grasp. He ran faster than before and soon could only hear The Kaiser's call on the wind.

"This is my land! My rats! You stay OUT!"

Chapter Twelve

No-Man's-Land

Eventually Tom came to a stop, his tiny lungs gasping for air. He had lost all sense of direction now – he was deep in no-man's-land with no hope of getting out. Not only did he have to avoid bullets and explosions, but now he had to steer clear of a violent German cat too. He was beginning to think all was lost.

"Stupid, stupid Tom!" he cursed himself. "Why did I think I could do this? I'm a farm cat. I'm no warrior!"

He looked about and saw no other souls near him. He had parted from the men and that meant that he was truly, unavoidably, absolutely lost.

"That's it then. Tom the farm cat dies on a battlefield – killed by his own stupidity."

There was a short moment of silence in the gunning and Tom listened. The air echoed with the sound of the last shot and Tom could hear the sound of birdsong briefly. He marvelled that once the sound of terror had been stripped away, the sounds of the countryside were still there, as they always had been.

Then he heard another sound.

"Hrrgh..."

He turned and kept low; the sound was familiar but he didn't now why. It could be danger.

"Hrrrrggh..."

He crept forward towards the sound, poking his head over a small mound.

"Hrrghhh- agh!"

He peeked over a tuft of grass to see two soldiers lying in the mud, gripping their rifles, out of breath. Under the metal helmet Tom could just make out a shock of bright ginger hair.

"Jim!" he chirruped.

"What on Earth...?" said Jim as Tom leapt over the mound to land on his chest.

"What the blazes? That bleedin' cat!" said Biggsy. He was next to Jim, his leg bleeding and wrapped in barbed wire. "Are you two joined at the hip or something?"

Jim laughed as Tom sat on him and rubbed his head over his friend's chest, purring.

"You daft moggy!" he chided. "How'd you get out here? We're miles from the trenches!" Tom stopped rubbing his head to stare deep into Jim's eyes. "You...you came for me, didn't you?"

A moment passed between the two of them which neither could understand nor describe. For that second, they were talking at a different level; they both knew what each other meant, and they were both saying *'I'm here for you.'*

"Ahem," coughed Biggsy. "I hate to break up the reunion, but I'm bleeding here."

Jim sat up carefully so Tom jumped off his chest. The young soldier pulled himself around to his friend's wounded leg, careful not to put his head up too high – he could never tell where an enemy sniper might be. He then pulled out a small pair of pliers.

"I knew these would come in handy the moment I saw that barbed wire," he said. "Always carried these at home, in case a sheep got tangled in the fences on the farm."

"Very clever," said Biggsy, wincing. "Now get that stuff off my leg."

Jim concentrated while he snipped around the leg. Wire pinged away from them as he cut it off, making Tom jump. Soon Biggsy was free, but his leg was badly cut.

"I'll bandage you up," said Jim. He tore off a length of bandage from his kit and wrapped it around the leg. Luckily none of the barbs had entered the skin too deep.

"All right, let's get out of here," said Biggsy. "Where the 'eck are we anyway?"

Oh good, it's not just me that's lost, thought Tom.

"Not a clue. I lost my bearings after that last shell hit," said Jim. "The big question is, what are we going to do about *you*, fleabag?"

Tom ignored the friendly insult and rubbed his head against Jim again.

"He's not coming with us!" said Biggsy. "He'll slow us down!"

Jim knew his friend was right, but also knew the strange feeling in his heart was not fear, but comfort.

"He's my lucky mascot," Jim said. "Remember when he saved me?"

"Remember we're in a war? We can't be looking out for a stupid cat!" Biggsy said. Jim gulped and waved his hand at Tom.

"Go! Go on! Hop it!" he shouted. Tom simply stood still with a puzzled expression on his face.

"No chance," mewed Tom. "I'm here to protect you, whether you like it or not."

Biggsy saw the stalemate and shook his head in disbelief.

"Come on, let's get to it. We're not looking out for 'im, mind. If he chooses to follow us, that's his own lookout."

Jim nodded, then winked to Tom.

On the count of three, the pair of privates rose from the mud and crept forward, guns in hand. Tom trotted behind, looking happy and carefree now he had tracked Jim down.

Biggsy was silent, looking all around him. The gunfire seemed to be sounding way off to their left.

"The battle's that way," said Biggsy. "We should join up with 'em." He seemed reluctant.

"We better hurry," said Jim. "That fog's rolling in. Soon we won't be able to see a thing." On the horizon a great mist was moving towards them.

Tom followed them quietly. He was well aware that Biggsy didn't want him to be there – in truth, Tom didn't want to be there himself. He had a promise to keep; he would look after Jim, and they'd both go back to Devon together.

Just then, Tom felt peculiar. He caught a whiff of something unpleasant and it made his whole body shake with fear. He wailed loudly.

"Shhh! Tom, keep it down! We...Tom?" Jim began. He stopped as he saw the cat moving strangely. He was jerking in fear, his tail stood on end. "Tom, what's the matter?"

"That's odd. Cats usually only do that when-" Biggsy paused, stopping dead in his tracks. He flashed a panicked look at Jim. "That's not fog..." he muttered, scared.

"GAS GAS GAS!" yelled Jim, as he reached for his mask.

Chapter Thirteen

Survive

Jim hastily grabbed his gas mask and began to fix the straps around his head. His hands shook as he pulled it over his ginger hair. *If you don't get it on right, you're a goner,* he thought, remembering the Captain's warning. He forced himself to stop and calm his shaking hand before continuing.

"Stupid bleedin' things!" yelled Biggsy as he fiddled with his own gas mask. "I can't get it on!"

Tom was coughing and running in circles in a panic, quite unaware of the danger of mustard gas but instead knowing deep down that a *bad thing* was coming. It was the same fear he felt when storms were on the horizon, or a large angry dog was loose in the next field back home.

"Don't just stand there!" Tom wailed to Jim. He couldn't understand why they both felt the need to put a strange hat on suddenly. "Move! Run!"

Jim finally had the mask fixed around the back of his head and pulled down with force, desperate to get the mouthpiece over his face. He heard a small crack and caught his breath as he saw the transparent viewing window shatter in front of him.

"No. No, no, NO!" he screamed. With a hole in the mask, it was useless. The gas would enter and kill him in seconds. He looked up and saw the gas rolling in on the gentle wind; a slow-moving killer.

"Run! Run!" mewed Tom again. Jim shot him a glare and shouted angrily.

"Come on then!" he yelled. "If you're such great luck, save me now!"

Tom was taken aback at the tone but knew what to do. Instinct kicked in and he ran away from the death-cloud, stopping at the base of a tree. He looked back and saw to his relief that Jim was following him. Biggsy however was far behind.

"Biggsy! This way!" called Jim.

But Biggsy had begun to breathe in the gas and was coughing violently. He ditched his gas mask and started to run towards Jim but the gas was already taking effect; his lungs has begun to fill with liquid. He was drowning on dry land.

"Climb!" Tom meowed and leapt up the first part of the trunk in one go. Jim looked between the cat and his friend, but Biggsy was already on his knees. Between gasps and coughs, he found the energy to saw a few final words.

"Run, you idiot..."

Jim forced himself to turn away from his fellow soldier and started to climb the tree. Dropping his heavy rifle in order to climb easier, he saw that growing up on an orchard had its advantages, one being that his tree-climbing skills were well developed.

Tom leapt from branch to branch, getting as high as the old tree would allow. Jim followed, slower but determined.

"This better work..." he muttered as he sat at the top of the tree. Soon he saw that it would. The cloud of yellow gas was heavy and low-lying, and passed underneath them as they sat on top of it. "How did you know it would save us?" he said to Tom.

"Search me," said Tom back with a meow. "That's instinct for you."

And it was. He had trusted his instinct and he had paid off once more. He had saved Jim's life. The only problem was that he had a feeling that it would not be the last time.

The gas passed.

When he saw the way was clear, Jim dropped to the ground and retrieved his rifle. Tom leapt down carefully, landing gracefully on four feet.

"You saved me again," said Jim quietly. He rubbed Tom's head roughly, causing the ginger cat to purr loudly. Jim then walked back to the place he had last seen his friend.

Biggsy lay face down in the mud. Jim could not see his face, which was probably just as well. He paused as he looked down at the body, unable to think about what had just happened. He knelt and fumbled in the pockets of Biggsy's uniform, helping himself to ammo before removing one of his identity tags.

"Let's go back," said Tom. "We can go back to the trench now. Back to Devon."

But Jim began to walk onwards, towards the gunfire in the distance.

"JIM!"

The cat's wail stopped Jim in his tracks. He turned to see Tom facing the opposite way and stared at him with an unreadable expression; his mind was in a daze.

"I can't go back," he said. "My orders were to advance."

Tom uttered another sharp wail of protest.

"I can't! You don't understand!" he said, shouting at Tom. "If I go back without an order to retreat, I could get shot for cowardice. Either way I'm dancing with death but at least if I press onwards I can die like a hero."

"You'll die like a fool!" said Tom. "Just like all the other soldiers." He spat and arched his back crossly.

Jim, tired and in shock, walked onward towards the battle. Tom looked at his friend and wanted to leave him to his silly war. He didn't understand; his friend had just died in front of him, but he wasn't showing any signs of sadness. He hated him at that moment; hated him for following orders blindly and for carrying on with the ridiculous battle. As he watched Jim walk away however, he felt a pull on his heart.

"Our connection is strong," Tom said. "I suppose I had better save him again."

He stood and walked on, following his friend further into the battle.

Chapter Fourteen

Standing Guard

Tom pressed on. The day was still young and the boy and his cat had walked into a valley shrouded in mist. It was definitely mist this time, as Tom could smell only dew and grass on the breeze, instead of life-choking gas.

"Mist is good," muttered Jim. "Gerry'll think they got us in the gas attack. If we come at 'em from out of the mist, they won't see us until it's too late."

He talked bravely but Tom saw a frightened little boy under the steel helmet. He had just seen a man die. His friend was gone. He was alone on a battlefield with only his rifle and his cat for company. He was shaken.

"Come on soldier!" said Tom, trotting up beside Jim and mewing sweetly. "You call that a march?"

Jim laughed as Tom dashed ahead a few feet and the two chased each other for a hundred yards. When he resumed his normal march, Jim pulled out a photo from his breast pocket and began to hum a tune.

"*Daisy, Daisy, give me your answer, do...*" he sang. "*I'm half crazy, hopeful in love with you! It won't be a stylish marriage, I can't afford the carriage. But you look sweet, upon the street, On a bicycle built for two...*"

He kissed the photo and Tom saw the image; his sweetheart Daisy, pretty in pigtails. He tucked it back into his pocket and looked down to Tom.

"Get me back home, Tom," he said. "I don't care how, just get me back."

They marched on in silence for a few seconds until the peace was broken by an all too familiar whistle in the air.

"It's a shell," Jim yelled. "Get down!"

Neither had time to react as the shell fell from the sky, exploding nearby. Mud flew up and Jim was catapulted through the air, landing in a heap a few yards away. Tom, many times lighter than his friend, was hurled further and landed in a pile of mud. He was a lithe cat and managed to land safely but not altogether gracefully. He toppled as he fell but as he still had the elasticity of a kitten, his bones remained unbroken. His breath was knocked from him and it took him a few moments to recover.

"Jim!" called Tom, his ears ringing from the blast. "Jim?"

He carefully stood and wobbled on his four paws. Dizzily he walked on, unsure of where to look for his friend. The scent of mud and smoke filled the air. He walked around in a circle and then zigzagged his way across the ground until he saw a boot sticking out from behind a mound.

"Jim, are you all right? I thought-" Tom began, but as he came around the mound he saw that Jim was not all right. He lay on his back as still as a statue, his eyes closed. Tom ran up to him in a panic and sniffed at his face which was blackened with soot and mud. "Please be okay, please be okay..."

As his whiskers touched Jim's top lip, he felt a small breath come from his nose. Unconscious but breathing. Sniffing around some more, Tom smelt a hot iron stench trickling down Jim's leg.

He's hurt. Tom thought. He saw a dark stain spread through Jim's green trousers but it didn't seem to be bleeding badly. Under Jim's thigh lay the source – a jagged shard of metal, probably from the shell that exploded, was wedged deep into his leg.

What do I do? Thought the small cat. *I can't get help. I can't leave him.*

Only then did it occur to him that he was a tiny cat in the centre of a very large human war. He was next to useless. Even if he could find the rest of the British soldiers, what would they think he was trying to tell them? No one understood him like Jim did.

So I stay. I stay with him until he wakes, he thought. *And hopefully he'll tell me what to do...*

And so the cat stayed. Sat next to the boy like a sentry, Tom licked himself clean to the sound of guns in the distance. He didn't know if he would be stuck there for hours or days, but he was prepared to stay for as long as it took.

Time passed and Tom rose to stretch his legs. The day had worn on and it was getting close to dusk. He paced a few steps and peered into the half-light.

Red eyes shone back.

Tom froze, his heart racing. He dropped his head low into the first part of his rodent catching routine, but knew that he didn't have the bravery to pounce. This was no mouse.

It was a rat.

Tom's instinct kicked in again and it told him to run – but this time he ignored it. While his fear of rats was great, his loyalty to Jim was greater and he stood his ground.

I should pounce, he thought, still frozen. *I know I should, but...I can't.*

The red eyes of the rat scuttled closer revealing the silhouette of its fat body. Tom had to act before it got closer to Jim.

"HISSSCCCKKK!" he spat, arching his back and sticking out his tail to make him look bigger. His fangs were bared and it did the trick – the rat ran away.

"I wouldn't do that if I were you..." came a voice from the darkness.

Tom looked about and saw a familiar black figure in the dusk. The Kaiser was back...

"You again," said Tom, trying hard to stop his voice from quivering. "What wouldn't *you* do?"

The Kaiser came closer.

"If you scare one away, they just return with more," he said. He sat on the ground and licked his paw. "The only real way to make sure they won't harm anyone is to kill them on the spot. But you won't do that, will you?"

Tom forced himself to meet The Kaiser's green eyes.

"What are you talking about?" said Tom.

"RATS! Rats, my dear. MY rats," said The Kaiser. Tom flinched at the word and cursed himself for doing so.

"If you want the rats so badly, go and kill 'em. You'd be doing us all a favour."

Tom stood his ground, Jim still lying still by his side.

"Believe me I would, but my skills would be wasted if I used my energies on any old rat," he said. "No, there is one I have my eye on. A real beast! He's strong and large and cunning. Rather like myself."

Tom sighed at The Kaiser's vanity.

"And you want to kill it?"

"That's right. I've seen it nearby. And I need you to go away."

Tom laughed. He hadn't meant to, and The Kaiser looked shocked.

"Sorry, it's just that...I can't leave. I need to look after him," he said, nodding to Jim. "He's hurt, you see?"

The Kaiser looked at the leg wound.

"Yes, which is exactly why I need you to leave," he said. "You see, I've tracked my rat for a while. He gets slower when he eats and his favourite food is meat. If he feasts on your boy there, I dare say he'll be sluggish enough for me to take him out."

It was Tom's turn to be shocked.

"But...Jim's *alive*."

"I'm sure the rat won't mind," said The Kaiser. His green eyes glinted as a flash lit up the horizon, a bomb exploding on the battlefield. "Can you do that for me?"

Tom stood on his paws and arched his back in anger.

"No. Jim is alive and no one will touch him. Not you, not your rat. NO ONE!"

The Kaiser remained still. He was not looking for a fight. At least, not just now.

"Very well. But you need to know something. That boy is not your friend. He is not your ticket home. He is *human*. And humans created this. This...*hell*," he said, looking around him. "I was like you once. A mouser in a grand country estate in Bavaria. But the war came and they dumped me in the trenches. I had been betrayed."

Tom relaxed, seeing that the large cat was not going to fight him. He continued his speech.

"I will die here. I know that now. And so will your soldier, and so will you. Humans brought you into this place, so think carefully who you are loyal to."

"I'm not letting that rat near him," Tom said.

"Fine. But if you kill it before me, you'll pay dearly." The Kaiser walked calmly away, leaving Tom on the battlefield, in the dark.

Chapter Fifteen

Protection

The night was cold. Tom was used to sleeping in barns and in the relative comfort of a dugout but night-time out in the open fields of no-man's-land was harsh. Thankfully there was no rain that night, but the wind whipped over the land from the east, the ice on the breeze cutting through Tom's insulating fur. To keep Jim warm he sat on his chest and curled up in a ball. A heavier cat may have crushed Jim's fragile rib cage, but tiny Tom weighed next to nothing.

The night was long. The darkness seemed to go on forever. What little sleep Tom managed to get was punctured with explosions from far away and dreams in which he ran through the meadows of Hill Farm again, chasing butterflies and rolling in the wheat. Until the dreamscape turned dark and the whistles of shells filled his mind until all he could hear, see and taste was war.

He awoke with a start. He could feel the shelling of his dreams creeping into reality and so shook himself awake.

For once, the night was silent. Eerily so, as Tom had never known a quiet night ever since he had arrived at the front line. He was instantly on alert.

Then suddenly a sound from his right. Not far away, he could hear the soft pad of a paw on mud. The Kaiser? No, too light. But not much.

Another sound. Far off, a shell whistled and Tom braced himself for the bang. It came, short and sharp, with a flash that lit up the sky for just a second. In that second, Tom saw a reflection of red eyes just yards away from him.

He saw a silhouette too, not of the rat he had scared away earlier, but another this time. A bigger rodent than he had ever seen before. A glint of sharp white teeth came from its mouth. Tom was in no doubt that this was the rat that The Kaiser had warned him of.

The Beast.

It was as large as Tom, if not bigger. Tom could tell it had been in a few fights in its life. The silhouette had revealed a chewed ear and logic told Tom that you didn't get to be that fat without fighting over a few dinners.

The flash of the explosion had died and Tom was left staring at the area of darkness where the Beast was – or had been.

The sound of paws padding in front of him told him the Beast was on the move. Not closer, but prowling around the still figure of Jim, lured by the scent of blood. Tom was frozen in fear, but desperately tried to talk himself out of it.

Do it, he told himself. *It's just a rat. A large mouse. You are quicker, sharper and better than that monster. Do it.*

But fear is illogical. Fear does not allow you to do something when it makes perfect sense to do it. Tom knew that he needed a special kind of feeling to spur him on. He needed *instinct*.

A squeak from his left made him turn quickly, jumping onto his paws and extending his claws so that they sunk down into Jim's chest. It was another rat, smaller and quicker but it must have sensed Tom's presence and kept its distance. For now.

Another squeak. Tom turned to the sound, where a different rat was padding around the still body of Jim. And another. And another.

He was surrounded.

Just then he heard a groan and a cough. Jim! The pain of Tom's claws on his chest had woken him slightly, but his body still needed rest so he fell back unconscious.

"Hm? Ur..."

It was not the most elegant sound but it was all Tom needed. The sound of his human had awoken the instinct within him.

He had to act and this time he knew why. He had to protect Jim. The boy had treated him well and he wanted to repay that kindness. He heard another whistle of a falling shell far away, and readied himself to strike.

Lock eyes.

He had no eyes to lock onto but he turned his body to the last place he had seen the Beast.

Sink low.

He dropped low, the muscles in his back legs taut and ready to strike. The whistle of the shell continued.

Wiggle bum.

He moved his rear end ever so slightly and waited for the flash of light to show him his quarry. The whistle faded and was quickly followed by a flash and boom of the shell landing.

POUNCE!

The Beast was lit up for just a second and Tom used the power of his instinct to leap, twisting his body to correct his position in mid air. He had misjudged the Beast's location by a few inches, but as he landed he thrust out his claws, digging deep into the rat's fur. There was a shriek from the Beast and the rest of the rats squeaked. Whether they were shouting in fear of Tom or in support of their friend was not clear, but Tom did not have time to worry about that.

He landed with a thud to the side of the great rat, who twisted and bit into the nearest part of Tom he could reach, his tail. It was Tom's turn to cry out as the pain shuddered through him, but he knew he could not rest. He leapt back and hissed. The Beast stood its ground.

The light from the explosion was fading so Tom leapt again, his claws extended and aimed at the Beast. As the light died, Tom could see the snarled lip of the rat and his razor sharp teeth as he fell on to him.

The Beast fought back, wriggling and tossing, attempting to throw Tom off him, but Tom held on for his life. He tried to use the same moves he would use to catch a mouse, but the size of the Beast made it impossible. He could only hold on and hope that his claws were doing the work for him. Another whistle and bang came from far off and Tom could see his prey once more, a face full of anger close to his.

He used the light to press down on the Beast's face and he bit into him hard. The rat struggled for a few seconds and then was still.

It was over.

Tom leapt from the still body of the Beast and let out a mighty yowl and hiss that told the rest of the rodents that their king was dead.

"Run away," he called to the army of rats who were already fleeing. "and never return."

He padded back to Jim, who was still unconscious. He stood next to his boy feeling happy in the knowledge that he had protected him well.

Over the horizon, the sun began to rise, casting a dim light over the battlefield and signalling a new day. As Tom lay his head on Jim's chest, he felt safe. Until he heard a voice in the half-light.

"Oh dear, oh dear..." came The Kaiser's meow. "I *did* try to warn you..."

Chapter Sixteen

Self-Preservation

The Kaiser walked towards Tom, slow and menacing.

"I told you not to trust humans," he said. "And then you go and protect one? You're more stupid than I thought."

"Back off," said Tom, his small voice not as threatening as he would have liked it to be. The Kaiser let out a hiss when he came upon the body of the Beast.

"My rat. You killed my rat!" he spat. "I told you he was MINE!"

"I don't take orders from you!" Tom spat back. He stood firm but was shaking underneath.

"Quiet, boy! This is MY land."

Tom took a step towards the large cat and dropped his head low, getting ready for a fight.

"Not anymore."

The Kaiser wasted no time with more threats and leapt on Tom, hissing and yowling. Tom was half his size but his youth meant he was quicker and more supple. He wriggled out from his grasp, not even feeling The Kaiser's claws as they dug into him.

Tom ran back but as The Kaiser ran towards him he twisted and dodged out of the way. The German cat landed in the mud and Tom used the brief moment of disorientation to pounce on him and bite into his back leg. The Kaiser howled and spat but managed to kick Tom off.

"You...you...you traitor!" shouted The Kaiser. "I am your kin! A mouser like you! You dare to bite *me*?"

Tom, breathless, shot a glare at the cat.

"You are no kin of mine..."

Then he charged. Tom rammed his head into the side of the large black cat which caused him to topple over on his injured leg. The Kaiser fell back, staggering and tumbling over into a pile of rusty barbed wire.

He screamed and leapt up as quickly as he could. His leg was caught and he managed to free himself in a few shakes, but the wounds were already apparent. Covered in cuts and bruises, he turned to stare at Tom.

"The battle's over..." he said, his voice cracking with pain and weakness. "But you haven't won the war yet, young Tom. Be careful..."

He turned and limped away into the sunrise. Tom walked to Jim and fell down on him, exhausted.*

"There's one!"

"Where?"

"There, by that mound. Grab a stretcher."

Tom woke to the sound of two men bickering as they crawled across the ground nearby. It was daytime, morning by the look of the sun peering through an overcast sky, and medics had been sent to retrieve the bodies and casualties of yesterday's big push. Tom was tired to the point that he did not even raise his head when they came near, but merely opened his eyes.

"Here, this one's alive!" said one of the medics. He was balding with a red face. "He's taken a battering though..."

"Can you hear me fella?" yelled the other man, younger and shorter. "We're going to get you back to base, straight to hospital. Looks like you've had a nasty trip!"

"I dunno, careless these young'uns ain't they?" laughed the balding medic.

They shifted Jim carefully and the pain of movement woke him for the first time in nearly twenty-four hours.

"Agh!" he yelled. "Tom! Tom?"

"Who's that then. That you?" said the shorter one.

"Nah, ID tag says he's a James," said Baldy. "That you? Jimmy? Who's Tom then? Your mate?"

Jim, despite his mind being in a fog from the pain, managed to answer.

"My cat..." he muttered. The medics laughed, but Tom heard his friend and sat up with a gentle chirrup.

"Well, blow me down..." said Shorty. "Has he been with you the whole time?"

Jim nodded and closed his eyes to rest. The medics looked at each other and shrugged.

"I suppose you're on our side," said Baldy to Tom. "Hop on then..."

He lifted the blanket that was covering Jim's legs and Tom did as he was told. They placed the blanket down and carried the stretcher back towards the front line.

By the time they were safe in their own trenches and headed towards the reserve trench on a cart, Jim was awake, but groggy after the medic had given him a shot of morphine to stop the pain.

"The cat...where is he?" said Jim, the world spinning around him.

"You won't feel him through the morphine, but he's there. Curled up under your cover, he is."

Jim smiled.

"He saved me," he said. The medic didn't seem to hear, so he said it again. "He saved me..."

"Is that right? Take on Gerry singled handed, did he? Or should that be single pawed?" Baldy laughed. Jim shook his head, then stopped as if the movement was making him feel dizzy.

"He stayed with me. He never left..." he said. He thought back to his promise to his feline friend and knew what he had to do. "Mate, I'm going to need your help..."

And so Tom became a refugee from the war. As Jim was transported to a field hospital he and the medic made sure that Tom was kept firmly under wraps. He remained under the cover until the nurses could sit Jim up enough for him to hide him under the bed.

"Keep quiet and we'll be back home in no time," said Jim. Tom seemed to understand and remained under the bed, spending the time licking his own wounds and recuperating. Jim slipped him some meat at dinnertime but he largely went unnoticed by the staff. The patients that were able to move about were let in on Jim's secret and helped the young lad to keep his cat hidden.

Tom did not like staying still but he knew that it was for the best. He would sneak out at night to prowl and take care of toilet duties, but for the most part he was happy to rest in his hiding hole. There was one day however when Jim was taken from his bed onto a stretcher and wheeled away. For hours Tom was alone in the ward, a few friendly patients checking on him now and again.

"He'll be back, little one," said a friendly captain. Half of his face was wrapped in bandages, a nasty burn underneath. "Just sit tight."

Eventually Jim was wheeled back and put into bed, just before lights-out.

"Jim!" Tom said, leaping out from under the bed. He jumped up and stood on his chest, sniffing his friend's face and rubbing against him. "You went away! Where did you go?"

Jim did not answer. Either he didn't know what Tom was trying to say or he did not want to answer. Tom looked around in the darkness and walked up and down the bed. Something was wrong. The bed felt strange...as though something was missing.

Jim sighed and pulled the blanket up for Tom to crawl under, which he did. It was then that Tom saw what was missing.

"I got gangrene, they said. They couldn't save it."

Tom crept down to the foot of the bed, where Jim's one remaining leg lay. He sniffed the stump of his left leg, wrapped in bandages and smelling of surgical alcohol.

"I've got to learn to walk with crutches, but otherwise I'll be fine," Jim said. "Thanks to you, Tom. You got me here. You kept me alive. You gave me hope."

Tom lay down and purred.

"I'm glad I could serve with you," he said, shutting his eyes; a cat's kiss.

"And every cloud has a silver lining," said Jim. "I ship out tomorrow. We're going home."

Chapter Seventeen

Homecoming

Tom had more hiding to do. Jim placed him in a dufflebag which he insisted on having with him at all times. If the nurses or ambulance men tried to take it he would clutch hold of it tightly and refuse to let go.

"I need that. Sentimental reasons," he said. If anyone tried to argue he would just show them the stump where his left leg used to be. "Give us a break, will you mate? I've been in the wars..."

After that they left him alone.

The crossing was choppy but Tom managed to sleep most of the way. It is the greatest skill of a cat to be able to sleep in the unlikeliest of locations and Tom was an expert at it; after nights in the trenches, a rocky channel crossing was a welcome quiet snooze.

After which Jim was sent to a convalescence home in England. He was given a bed in a grand country house somewhere in Surrey with sunny gardens to practise his crutch skills. Tom resumed his hiding routine until one day he was discovered by a shrieking nurse.

"Aaagh! It's a rat!" she called as she flung back the covers to bath an unsuspecting Jim. "Matron!"

"How rude!" said Tom, standing up and stretching. "And when have you ever seen a *ginger* rat?"

Matron came running, Jim already protectively putting his hand over Tom.

"I can explain..." he began, but Matron, a fussy round woman with her hair in a bun, talked over him.

"This is a centre for medicine! Not a home for waifs and strays! That...*thing* will have to be removed at once."

"Over my dead body!" retorted Jim. They called a doctor to police the stand off between them. Jim told them everything; how Tom had saved him that first time in the trenches, their life together on the front line, the journey through no-man's-land and the care Tom had shown for him since.

"Remarkable," said the doctor. He was a handsome man in his fifties. The war had turned his hair grey with worry for his patients. "Such unusual loyalty for a cat." He stroked Tom and gave Jim a wink. "Keep him clean, make sure he exercises and gets out to the toilet at least once a day and I'm sure we won't have a problem here."

"I will, Doctor. Thank you," smiled Jim.

"I was talking to the cat," the doctor joked.

And so Tom became a fixture at the convalescence home, making more friends with the soldiers. The doctor noticed a marked improvement in morale among the men after they were allowed to pet young Tom and was sorry to see Jim and his furry friend leave.

"It's time to get back home," said Jim as he climbed into the back of the army truck which would take them back to Devon. A selection of patients and staff looked on, giving Tom a final stroke. "What about it Tom? Ready to see the red hills of home again?"

"Yes!" Tom mewed loudly. Their audience laughed and applauded as Tom made the tall leap up to the truck in one bound. "Take me home!"

*

The truck rumbled to a stop and the driver jumped out of the cab to open the back.

"Are you sure I can't take you all the way to the farm, Jim?" said the driver. "It's no trouble. I don't want you getting stuck in the mud with that leg of yours."

"It's all right Benny. I walked away on my own. I want to walk back too," said Jim. He grabbed the driver's hand and jumped down to the ground, wobbling on his good leg. Tom stretched and leapt down too, a tad easier.

"Stay lucky," said Benny as he patted Jim on the back, before driving away.

Jim looked at the gate to his father's farm for a spell, remembering the peeling dark green paint and the smell from the orchard. He leaned on his crutches, readying himself to move.

"Well," he muttered to Tom. "You got us back all right. I know I said to get me home no matter what, but I was expecting to keep all my limbs..."

"Beggars can't be choosers," said Tom.

Tom sniffed the air. Somewhere a joint of beef was cooking, probably over at Jim's farmhouse. He knew he had waited for so long to get back to the place where he was born and that he would be accepted as one of the family at Jim's farm, but for some reason he found the idea of walking through that gate...wrong. He loved Jim. Jim, finally, was home. But it wasn't *Tom's* home.

"Come on then," said Jim. He moved forward on his crutches to the gate and leaned on it while he lifted the catch. Tom remained still. "You coming?"

He couldn't. He wanted to, but he couldn't. He had to get home and see Jezebel, Stanley and Old Jack. He wanted to jump about in the fields he grew up in and chase butterflies. He wanted to sort out the rats once and for all and show the crows what he had learned while he was off at war.

"You...you're not coming, are you?" said Jim. His heart sank in his chest a little.

"I...I'm sorry..."

Jim crouched down and sat on the ground next to the gate. Immediately Tom jumped on him and rubbed him with his head, purring uncontrollably. Jim kissed him and stroked him, holding back tears.

"You've been the best friend I could ever imagine," he said. "You got me through the war. You got me home."

"And you've been a soul mate," said Tom in purrs. He looked up and kissed Jim on the face with his cold, wet nose, drinking in his familiar scent. Jim could hold back the tears no longer, but laughter came with them, great sobs and giggles at the same time. Eventually after a moment of silence between them, Jim stood and Tom leapt from his lap.

"Go on then," he said with a sigh, wiping his eyes. "If I'm right about your ID tag, your home is somewhere over the hill. Few miles. Be careful."

Tom looked at him quizzically.

"We survive the war and only *now* you tell me to be careful?" He mewed. "I'm not the one who lost his leg..."

Jim turned and opened the gate, hopping through it with his crutches in one hand and steadying himself with the other. He swung the gate closed and leaned on it while he positioned his crutches.

"Have a good life, Tom Hill."

And so the boy and his kitten were now separated, but they had grown into a man and his cat. Tom looked at the gate opposite Jim's farm and the meadow beyond. He didn't know how but he just *knew* that this was the way home. It was a feeling in his tummy that told him to walk on and follow his heart and then everything would be all right.

I've felt this feeling before. What is it? thought Tom. *Ah, yes. Instinct.*

Climbing through the fence posts, Tom ran onward though the meadow of grass and poppies, back home.

Afterword

Animals played a key part in the First World War. It is estimated that 16 million animals were used, from pigeons and dogs to transport messages, to horses and camels to transport goods and people.

Cats were used mainly as pest control to kill the rats and other vermin that plagued the trenches. They were also an early warning sign for gas attacks. Many were adopted as mascots and were company for the men that fought in the trenches.

In 1943 the Dickin Medal was set up by the founder of pet charity PDSA to honour animals who have served in the armed forces and shown great bravery. In the years between 1943 and 1949 it was awarded to 32 pigeons, 18 dogs, 3 horses... and a cat.

Glossary

Ammo/Ammunition – Supplies of bullets, grenades etc.

Artillery – Large guns used to fire at the enemy

Barbed Wire – Wire with sharp pieces of metal attached.

Bayonet – A large blade fitted on the end of a rifle for hand-to-hand fighting.

Bully Beef – Corned beef

Captain – A rank in the army above Lieutenant

Commanding Officer /C.O. - Officer in charge of a Battalion.

Convalescence – Recover from an illness or injury

Feet/Foot – Imperial unit of measurement consisting of twelve inches – equal to around thirty centimetres.

Front Line – The boundary where each side in the war faced each other.

Gerry – Slang term for German soldiers.

Grenade – Exploding weapon thrown by a soldier

Inch – Imperial unit of measurement. Equal to around two and a half centimetres

Kaiser – The German Emperor

Land mine – Explosive buried in the ground and designed to detonate when stepped on.

Medic – Soldier trained to give some medical help.

No-man's-land – Area of land between the two front lines; territory unclaimed by either side in the war.

Pineapples – Slang term for grenades, named after the fruit they looked like.

Private – Lowest rank in the army

Quarry – Something that is hunted.

Sergeant/Sarge – A rank in the army above Corporal.

Shell – A hollow missile containing explosives.

Shrapnel – Pieces of metal spread by exploding bombs.

Sniper – A soldier who shoots at the enemy from a hiding place.

Stand-to – A shortening of 'Stand to arms', the order shouted to soldiers to stand at their positions and get ready to fire.

Tommy – Slang term for British soldiers.

Trench – A deep ditch

Yard – An imperial unit of measurement consisting of three feet. Equal to around ninety centimetres.

About the Author

Dan Metcalf is the author of children's books such as *The Lottie Lipton Adventures, Jamie Jones: Galaxy Defender (Aged Eight and a Half), Codebusters* and *Dino Wars.*

He gained a BA (Hons) in Scriptwriting for Film and Television at Bournemouth University and in 2016 his pilot script for the children's drama *Locksley*, based on the early life of Robin Hood, was chosen to appear on the BAFTA Rocliffe Children's Media Shortlist.

A former bookseller and librarian, he lives in Devon with his wife and two sons and has so far absolutely refused to grow up.

Find him online at www.danmetcalf.co.uk

31750740R00085

Printed in Poland
by Amazon Fulfillment
Poland Sp. z o.o., Wrocław